The Revenge of Blood-Red Rivers

Martin Lundqvist

Published by Martin Lundqvist, 2021.

This is a work of fiction. Similarities to real people, places, or events are entirely coincidental.

THE REVENGE OF BLOOD-RED RIVERS

First edition. February 8, 2021.

Copyright © 2021 Martin Lundqvist.

Written by Martin Lundqvist.

Chapter 1: The calm before the storm; March 1994.

When I close my eyes, I can still envision those distant days in March '94, albeit my memory has faded over the years.

"Samantha, come and play soccer with us." My brother always joked. Sometimes I obliged, and he always laughed in glee at my clumsiness with the soccer ball, as he was running laps around me. This took place in the soil field next to the river where the children of our village met.

"Yuhi, stop being mean to me!" I remember shouting at my brother. I remember the look of the old worn-out ball, the earthy mud fields and warm rivers, but I cannot remember the face of my brother, just glimpses of a happier time. When I think of my dear brother, I only remember his happy smile, his cute innocence and thundering laughter whenever he scored a goal. It was always a debate between us whenever someone scored a goal, as we didn't have proper goal posts to determine who was the real winner. We used our worn-out shoes as goal posts and played barefoot instead. This was crucial not to break our old and much-loved shoes any further. They were the only ones that we've got, and we needed the shoes for when we helped our parents ploughing the farmlands, to avoid stepping on rocks, or walking on venomous animals. Our school's sports field was clear of sharp rocks, so why would we wear out our shoes when playing barefoot worked just as well?

I remember coming home after a day in school, which was followed by fishing in the muddy warm river with my dad. We ate umitsuma, a mixed of cassava and corn for lunch and dinner. This was our daily staple. We rarely ate meat, except when one of us were lucky enough to catch a fish or a bird. Our days were joyful; we were poor but at least our poverty brought us together. It was not at all like the cool and modern suburbia I am now living in, after I escaped to Australia as a Rwandan genocide survivor.

Occasionally, my father would gently whisper to us about the current news from the rest of Rwanda. Our family didn't have a TV. We did not even have a radio, but we did know how to read, so we followed the headlines in the newspapers that they sold in a nearby town. Sometimes me or my brother would run to the neighbouring town and pick up old newspapers and books from the rubbish bins. It was too wasteful to buy today's newspaper when old newspapers gave us the same opportunity to read and learn about the world in different languages. On a good day, I found old newspapers or books in Kinyarwanda, French, or English. I loved learning different languages of the world, and I often would imagine myself travelling to these places that they spoke about in books. My brother Yuhi found my fascination with languages to be silly. "How often do you ever speak to someone who doesn't know Kinyarwanda? The white man never comes here anyway."

"Don't be ignorant, Yuhi. Samantha's desire to amass knowledge will make our village proud one day. We are the Nyamwasa family, and we have always valued knowledge." My father, Mutara Nyamwasa, replied kindly.

"I guess books are good for her since she won't be a professional footballer when she grows up," Yuhi smirked and ran off to play some more football, as usual.

When Yuhi had ran away, I spoke to my dad about something that I read in the newspaper. "Father. The newspaper said that President Juvénal Habyarimana is facing difficulties with the peace treaty. Why is that? Why can't people live in peace?"

Mutara gave me a worried expression and explained, "That is because the devil and evil spirits influence people to want discord. It's the way of the world. You can only make things better by helping the good spirits around you."

"But will we be safe?" I asked innocently.

"Man cannot know his fate. Only our God Jesus Christ knows. To speculate on these matters is a waste of energy. We must pray that God will save us and things will work out." My father said with a kind but worried voice.

Looking back at our talk, I believe that our father had a lack of foreboding suspicion of what was about to happen. While a part of me is blaming him for not taking precautions, another part of me understands him. We cannot let fear govern our lives. My father's lack of preparation is also understandable, as our part of the country was never involved in the civil war that ravaged the northern parts of Rwanda between 1990 to 1993. Yet, after the short-lived peace, the worst was about to come.

Looking back, I also recall a conversation I had with my mother, Junema, a short while before everything fell apart.

"Why can't I have another sibling, mother? Ours is the smallest family in the village." I pleaded.

"I am not sure, my dear child. We have been praying to Jesus Christ every night for another child, but we have not been blessed." My mother replied solemnly. I joined my mother in praying for another sibling that night, but nothing happened. In retrospect, I have realised that my mother and I were genetically predisposed to the same condition, with one dissimilarity. She had two children before she got old enough for the condition to appear.

Chapter 2: Blood-red rivers; April 1994.

I remember the day it all started. It was a Sunday morning, and I wanted to go to the neighbouring town and get some old newspapers after having attended Sunday Mass. My father had reprimanded me with a fit of surprising anger. "No, Samantha. I forbid you from leaving the village. Go catch a fish in the river. I am hungry."

My father's anger had puzzled me. He had always said that the hunger for knowledge was more important than the hunger of the flesh. Why had he changed his mind? I didn't want to anger my father in my pursuit of knowledge, so I decided to grab a fishing net and try to catch a fish in the nearby muddy river instead.

As I stood in muddy waist-deep water, I reflected over how the colour of the water was gradually changing, from a brown reddish hue, ever so-slowly to bright alarming red. I assume this was a minor concern at a time, as I was so young and innocent, but in retrospect, I wish I had warned everyone there and then. After several fruitless hours, I finally caught something big and heavy in my fishing net.

At first, I felt instant joy. A fish this big could feed the whole village, I thought to myself. But then I felt something strange. Why wasn't the fish struggling when I reeled in the net? I knew that we were not supposed to eat fish that was already dead when we caught it, but I wanted to make my dad happy and proud of me.

As I pulled in the motionless "fish", I was hit with a horrific image of what was to be the worst incidence in my life which I remember till this day. I had caught the dismembered head of a man. I recognised the man, it was Kagabo from the neighbouring village. I panicked and ran away in terror, and the net which encapsulated the motionless head flowed downstream.

I ran to my father and screamed: "Father!! I caught Kagabo's head in the river. He is dead, Papa!"

My father gave me a disbelieving stare and replied. "Stop talking nonsense, Samantha. I know you are angry about having to fish on a Sunday, but it's unfair to the other children in this village if you don't do your part of the chores."

"Please papa. Come with me to the river and I'll show it to you." I pleaded. My dad sighed and followed me to the river, while muttering some grumbles.

As we got to the river, he gave me a stern look and asked: "Where is the fishing net, Samantha?"

"I dropped it and it followed the stream." I snivelled and I saw how my dad held back his anger.

I felt ashamed. My father wasn't a mean man, but we were poor, and we couldn't afford to lose the fishing net. "Sorry, papa. I will follow the river until I find the net." I apologised.

"Good. Be home before nightfall. There won't be dinner for you unless you bring the net back." My father scorned me.

I looked at him with teary eyes and started walking downstream. In retrospect, I realise that the reason why I have father issues is because our last encounter was so negative. Yet, it was this encounter that saved my life as I was away from the village when the massacres began.

. . . .

MANY HOURS LATER, I was on my way back to the village. I was tired and hungry, and my eyes were droopy and teary. I hadn't been able to find the lost fishing net, and I worried that my father would hit me. Getting scolded on an empty stomach was not the ideal way to spend a night, especially since I was only twelve years old.

As I approached the village, I heard loud screams and a group of men chanting. I didn't recognise their voices, which felt odd as we rarely had outsiders visiting our village. As I walked towards my hut, a man grabbed me from behind and put a hand on my mouth.

"Sssshh, be quiet if you want to live!" The man hissed sternly. I felt petrified, and despite my efforts, I couldn't break free from the strong hold of the man. I looked at the man's outfit, he wore military pants with a large blood-soaked machete hanging by his side. After a while, a group of army men led a group of women in chains past us, not knowing that we were there. I saw the leader of the group sitting in a jeep that moved in walking pace. "That's Colonel Patrick Bagosora. He is the commander of our unit and the one who ordered us to attack your village."

I don't know what got into me, but I tried to memorise Patrick's face and uniform as hard as I could. I guess that I already back then, in my terrified state, wanted to get revenge on the man who was responsible for the murder of my entire family.

As the army group moved away, my captor took his hand off my mouth and spoke. "We need to go to the village and look for supplies. We have a long walk ahead of us."

I nodded, sobbed, and said "Where are we going, and what's your name?"

The man gave me a cold stare and replied. "Don't ask questions, stupid girl. I am the one in control."

"Sorry. I'm Samantha Nyamwasa, and I just need a friend." I stuttered.

"Okay. My name is Phillippe, and I am taking you to safety far away from here." Phillippe replied.

"I need to see my family. We must help them." I pleaded.

"I'd rather not take you," Phillippe said sternly.

"Please. Otherwise, I won't go with you." I begged.

After muttering some profanities, Phillippe agreed to my desperate pleas. As we reached my hut, I saw my father dead outside the entrance. They had chopped him many times with machetes. My brother was the next family member I saw. They had tied him around an electricity pole, and used him as an archery target. I entered inside the hut, where I saw my mother lay naked on the ground with her eyes gouging out in terror. She was bleeding from several deep cuts to her legs, and someone had shattered a glass bottle and stuffed it into her vagina.

"Samantha, I am so glad to see you alive. You must get yourself to safety." Junema spoke in agony while gasping for the last breath of air. "Mama, who did this to you?" I cried.

"Patrick Bagosora, the nephew of Théoneste Bagosora. He murdered your father, and he made me watch as his men shot arrows towards your brother. After that, he raped me. He finished by shoving a broken glass bottle up my vagina." Junema whispered while falling in and out of consciousness.

I turned to Phillippe and cried: "We must get my mother to the hospital!"

He shook his head and replied. "No. The closest hospital is 30 kilometres away and she would bleed out on the way there. Besides, there is no help for someone like her at the hospital. President Juvénal Habyarimana is dead. Interim President Théoneste Bagosora has ordered the elimination of all Tutsis in this region. You can choose to let her bleed out or end her suffering right now."

I looked at my dear and pitiful mother, who was shaking in extreme agony and pain while passing in and out of consciousness. I could not let her die like this. "I'll do it," I said as I grabbed my mother's pillow while crying wildly. I placed it over her head, applied pressure with one hand while holding her hand until her weak pulse was gone.

I took the pillow away from her head. At the age of twelve, I had put my mother out of her misery and as I heard her last dying breath, I vowed to avenge my family. Patrick Bagosora would have to suffer for what he had done to the people of my village and my family.

Chapter 3: Rapists on the forest path; April-May 1994.

We were walking eastwards along the Lake Muhazi. I had done this walk once before, precisely two years earlier when my family had wanted to hike around the lake as a fun family experience. Back then, it had been a beautiful stretch of lush green grass mixed with welcoming rural villages and its warm and friendly people. I remember my papa telling me that the hiking track used to be even better before the civil war started, however, when I did the walk the first time it was still enjoyable.

My walk along the lake in April 1994 was anything but enjoyable. I was spending many days walking in the extreme heat with the curt and temperamental Phillippe, whose real motivation for bringing me along I hadn't figured out yet. Phillippe still wore the uniform of Théoneste Bagosora's Interahamwe Hutu militia that had pledged to exterminate my people. Yet his desire to murder people of the Tutsi tribe seemed to have subsided and had been replaced by the desire to take me to an undisclosed location.

The last day we walked along the lake before turning southeast, I had an episode of sickness that I will never forget. I was severely dehydrated as we hadn't been able to find a water source that wasn't contaminated with blood and human remains. I collapsed, and I yearned to drink from the pool of water that was only a few meters away from me. Yet the thought of drinking water contaminated with human remains sickened me even further, and I vomited violently.

"What's wrong, little girl?" Phillippe taunted.

"I need water. I am so weak." I replied meekly.

Phillippe gave me a sour look, threw his empty canteen bottle at me, and shouted, "I don't even have water for myself. We got to keep moving. There is an untainted water source a few hours walk away."

"How do you know?" I asked softly.

"I was with Interahamwe. I know where I can get water. Do you think we are stupid enough to contaminate our water source? Do you think we are stupid monkeys?" Phillippe taunted.

"I didn't. I am just thirsty." I mumbled.

"You've implied it, you rotten Tutsi cockroach. Apologize now!" Phillippe demanded.

"I am sorry, Phillippe." I sobbed.

"Get up. We need to move." Phillippe ordered.

I tried to get up on my feet, but my legs would not carry me, and I collapsed to the ground like an abandoned sack of corns. Phillippe swore and started kicking violently towards a tree, presumably instead of kicking me. Eventually, he made a fire, filled a cooking pot with unclean water, and started boiling it.

"The contaminated water won't kill you if you boil it first," Phillippe explained coldly.

"Thank you, Phillippe," I whispered weakly.

As Phillippe was boiling the water, two militiamen approached us. The taller of them spoke: "Hey soldier, why are you here, and why are you boiling this filthy water? There is freshwater an hour away."

"The girl. She is weak and refuses to get up unless I give her water." Phillippe replied.

"Bullshit. Why are you going alone with a girl in the forest anyway?" The militiaman asked.

"I am taking her to a buyer in Nyakasanza for Colonel Patrick Bagosora," Phillippe replied.

"Bullshit. The Colonel and his troops are leading a group of captured women to Kigali, to entertain our president. Why would he send you alone with this girl to Nyakasanza?" The shorter man disputed. "I don't know, dog. Why don't you ask him?" Phillippe mocked.

The taller man walked up to me, lifted me to a standing position, and inspected me. As he stared into my eyes with his black evil eyes, I knew that he was going to rape me. He pushed me to the ground and spoke. "I like this girl. If you let me take a ride on her, I will give you fresh water from our spring. How about that?"

"No. I won't let you damage the merchandise. The girl is worthless to me if you spoil her." Phillippe exclaimed.

The man showed Phillippe an evil grin and replied. "So, you haven't raped this girl yet? Even better, I'd love to be the first."

"No, I won't let you," Phillippe exclaimed and chested up against the taller man.

"Try to stop me," The man said and punched Phillippe, who fell backwards and hit his head.

The two Interahamwe men kneeled next to me and laughed. The taller man said: "Don't be afraid, little girl. You're about to become a mature woman, and that's a good thing. It would be a shame for a pretty thing like you to die a virgin."

After saying this, the man started pulling my clothes and undressing me. I felt very frightened but I was cold and frail, so I was powerless to resist. I punched the man a few times, but my arms lacked strength and the man didn't flinch. Quite the opposite, the more I resisted, the more excited he became, and I knew that he would soon enter me as they had done to my poor mother. Time slowed down, and I prayed to Jesus that I would die a quick and painless death. I had seen how my mother suffered after Patrick Bagosora raped her, and I didn't want that to happen to me. The man pulled off my panties, and my body stiffened from the dreadful sensation of the man forcing his manhood upon my frail and skinny body.

The rape was never completed. Instead, blood splashed all over my body as a terrifying scream of shock filled the forest. I looked up, and I saw Phillippe decapitate my rapist's head, then chopping the other man to pieces with his machete. I closed my eyes in horror of the image that I just saw, but felt relieved that the rape ordeal has ended, pushed the dead man away and passed out instantly.

• • • •

"DID HE MANAGE TO BREAK your virginity?" Phillippe asked with a cold and distant voice.

I shook my head. Phillippe smiled and replied: "Good, so you are still pure."

I took a deep breath. The thirst that had seared my throat before was now becoming more tolerable, and I felt that my collapse and unconsciousness had somehow replenished my energy.

Phillippe spoke, "You should drink and eat. I gave you some water while you were delirious, but we waste less water if you drink while conscious."

"So, do we have food and water now?" I asked softly.

"Yes. Those men that I killed had brought some supplies. We have enough food, water, and money for our trip to Tanzania now." Phillippe replied.

"So, why did you kill those men?" I asked.

"It was not me that killed them, it was God that killed those men. Why else would he had put them on our path?" Phillippe replied.

I didn't reply to Phillippe's statement. If there was a God, why had he allowed this terrible plight to happen on my people in the first place? We had walked past several Tutsi villages in the last week. They were all destroyed, with their inhabitants slaughtered and left to rot in the sun. Why would God allow such reckless hate to take place in this kind and loving world?

"We need to get moving. It's still many days walk to Nyakasanza in Tanzania." Phillippe stated.

"What's awaiting us in Tanzania?" I asked.

"For you, a clean and warm place in United Nations refugee camp. For me, a reward for bringing you there." Phillippe replied.

"Thank you for looking after me," I said and sought eye contact with the lone militiaman, who risked his life to keep me safe.

Phillippe didn't reply. Instead, he looked away and started walking on the path that took us to the southeast, in the direction of the Tanzania border. In retrospect, I have understood that Phillippe felt ashamed about his real intentions towards me. While I could hate him as much as I hate Patrick Bagosora, I never have. Because although Phillippe's intentions towards me were to trade me for money, they ended up being what brought me out of Rwanda alive.

Chapter 4: United Nations peacekeepers, a false hope; May 1994.

We were outside the town of Rusumo, located in south-eastern Rwanda, when I tried to escape from Phillippe. I ran towards a group of United Nations peacekeepers, who were handing out supplies to the throngs of refugees. We were following the path of countless others, we were following the highway to the Tanzanian border, just 20 kilometres to the south.

I had almost reached the soldiers wearing the blue helmets when Phillippe grabbed me from behind. He covered my mouth with one hand and growled: "What are you doing, stupid girl? Is this how you reward me for saving your life?"

Phillippe shook me and gave me a death stare. Once he had ascertained that I wouldn't scream, he took his hand off my mouth.

"You told the Interahamwe men that you would sell me to a buyer in Tanzania..." I sobbed.

"I also killed those men to stop them from raping you. Keep that in mind, that I am capable of murder." Phillippe warned.

I didn't reply and I sobbed in silence, while Phillippe was muttering an array of curses towards me.

We got back to our senses when we heard a loud ruckus nearby. Interahamwe soldiers had arrived in the town and I saw how they walked up to the UN soldiers. A line of militiamen walked up to within a metre of the UN camp and gave the peacekeepers a stare-down. A few minutes of tense silence ensued.

I felt surprised when I saw a limousine that carried the seal of Rwanda's presidential office drove up the UN outpost. The car stopped, and I saw a familiar face that stepped out of the car. Out of the car came Patrick Bagosora and a slightly older man, who I later recognised as Théoneste Bagosora, the architect behind the Rwandan genocide. Patrick walked up to the United Nations peacekeepers and spoke into a megaphone.

"Why are you here, foreign white dogs? Why are you objecting to the Hutu race reclaiming our country from our ancient Tutsi enemies? Go home!"

The UN commander replied something that I couldn't hear, and Patrick turned to the crowds. "Why do you turn to the disgraceful UN dogs for support?

They are cowards and won't do anything for you. Soldiers and my fellow Hutu people, witness how I force my manhood upon these Tutsi whores."

A few soldiers dragged a screaming woman to Patrick's side. They held her down over a table, while Patrick stripped her bare naked through cutting her clothes with his machete.

"We need to go now; this will turn ugly." Phillippe whispered and dragged me towards the scrublands at the edge of the village.

"Hey, where are you taking that girl?" an Interahamwe officer shouted as he intercepted us close to the edge of the town.

"I claim this Tutsi whore for myself. I will give her the best and the last fuck of her life." Phillippe said to the man.

The officer gave Phillippe a look of disgust and replied, "You are claiming this skinny kid when the town is full of mature women. You're a sick bastard."

"My preferences are none of your business. At least I can get it up, which is why I am claiming what I deserve instead of guarding the perimeter." Phillippe mocked.

A tense moment ensued, and in my mind, it seemed to drag on forever. What was Phillippe doing? He was either brave or insane to insult an officer. I feared that I would be the next unlucky woman to be dragged to the UN camp where Patrick was raping a woman in front of the crowd to mock the UN peacekeepers.

The soldiers cheered as Patrick lifted the severed head of the woman he had raped to the sky.

Phillippe used the distraction and dragged me away from the militiaman who impeded our progress. As we reached the forest, he whispered "Run," and we ran to the south, away from the town where the screaming and gunfire intensified.

· · · ·

"BLOODY LIMP DICK!" Phillippe mumbled as we were having a break a few kilometres from the Tanzanian border.

"Huh?" I asked.

"The officer that tried to stop us in Rusumo. I knew that he was a limp dick. I could tell from watching him." Phillippe taunted.

"What are you talking about? Shouldn't we figure out how to cross the border?" I asked.

Phillippe leaned over and slapped me. As I flinched and fell to the ground, Phillippe replied: "Don't tell me what to do, Samantha."

I didn't say anything, out of fear from angering Phillippe. We were so close to safety, only a few kilometres from the Tanzanian border, and I wouldn't throw away my life by angering my captor.

Phillippe continued his ramblings. "When a new soldier joins Patrick Bagosora's squad, he is expected to rape a Tutsi woman in front of his peers. If you fail, your peers consider you a limp dick, and you get to guard the perimeter while the others are having fun. That's how I knew how to get past the officer that stopped us at the edge of the village."

I didn't know how to respond to this statement. Phillippe hadn't shared much about his life, but I knew he had been guarding the perimeter when he caught me. I had also heard his tormented screams when he was having nightmares.

A part of me wanted to reach out to Phillippe and comfort him to ease his suffering. He wasn't less of a man for failing to rape someone in front of a crowd, quite the opposite, it made him a human. Yet, his failure as a rapist didn't make him a good man. A good man would never join a militia that aimed to rape and murder the Tutsis in the first place. My father was a good man. He would never have sunk that low.

"Fucking ugly bitch. Why did they give me such an ugly whore?" Phillippe muttered.

I felt terrified but I didn't say anything. Phillippe was volatile and the humiliating event in Rusumo had scarred his ego. In the worst-case scenario, he would try to rape me to get over his earlier shortcomings.

"Fucking ugly whore!" Phillippe exclaimed as he started chopping at a tree with his machete.

I looked at Phillippe as he was swinging at the tree. He looked feverish and very ill. Was this mental illness or was it something contagious? In any case, I feared more of what would happen in the near future, rather than the fear of catching a disease.

I went down on my knees and started praying to Jesus Christ. It was the first prayers I had uttered since the attack on my village. God had abandoned my village and condemned my family, so what was the point of living? I pushed aside my doubts. I was still alive, and God could help me. He had to help me. I couldn't die here. If I did, who would ever tell the story of my village and carry the memories of the fallen ones?

I don't know whether it was divine intervention, or just random occurrences, but after I had recited a few prayers, Phillippe collapsed to the ground in exhaustion. He shook uncontrollably and tears were running down his eyes. I hesitated, but I decided to go over to him, hold his hand, and wiped away his tears. Empathy was the only way to deal with people who are mentally unstable and filled with violent outbursts. It was the only way for our country to ever heal. However, there was one man who would never receive my empathy. I would kill Patrick Bagosora for what he did to my family!

Chapter 5: Crossing the border; May 1994.

I still have a large scar on my right arm where the crocodile bit me. I guess I am lucky that the crocodile was still juvenile, and that Phillippe knew how to fight it with his machete.

We had been walking along the highway and we were facing the bridge over the Kagera River that constituted the border to Tanzania. On the other side of that bridge, I would find relative safety, out of reach from the genocidal Interahamwe militia. There was, however, one problem. The Interahamwe had set up a roadblock near the border-crossing, and they murdered everyone that couldn't disprove their Tutsi heritage. They had piled up hundreds of corpses and the stench was unbearable. In retrospect, I have understood that the militias' lack of organisation was the reason they lost the civil war a few months later. Say what you want about other genocidal regimes, but most of them have enough sense to bury their victims, as bodies left in the open to rot will infect the perpetrators as well as the locals with dangerous diseases.

"Don't look so afraid. You are giving us away. A proud Hutu woman would rejoice at the sight." Phillippe whispered and grabbed my arm as I stared in terror at the many dead bodies laid upon each other.

As we walked away from the roadblock, I considered Phillippe's statement. Was the average Hutu person that heartless, or was it a tiny minority of the Hutus that caused all the terror, and forced the others to comply? Before the war, most of our neighbouring villages had been inhabited by Hutus. While we hadn't mixed with a lot with them, we had never faced any racial hostilities.

I followed Phillippe a few kilometres downstream, where we were safe from the stench of death and the murderous militiamen. At a stretch where the river was narrower, Phillippe stopped.

"We need to cross the river. This should be a good spot." Phillippe said.

I recalled the many crocodiles I had seen along the river and protested. "But Phillippe. There are a lot of crocodiles around here."

"Crocodiles are not as dangerous as Interahamwe militia. Crocodiles kill because they need to eat. Interahamwe on the other hand, kills to feed an insatiable hunger." Phillippe stated.

I reflected over Phillippe's statement. He was correct. No other animals were as despicable as humans. No other animal could have caused the carnage that took place in my country.

"Do you know how to swim?" Phillippe asked.

I nodded.

"Then we'll cross the river here. You'll go first." Phillippe commanded.

I stared at the river in terror, and I froze in place. Phillippe was right, but my fear of becoming crocodile food had triggered my primal fear response. This fear prevented me from entering the water.

"The militia is coming. Hurry up." Phillippe exclaimed.

Phillippe's words got me moving and I ran into the murky water, facing an uncertain future to avoid certain death. As the water reached my chest, I felt a sharp pain from a bite, followed by the shock when my shoulder dislocated, as a crocodile pulled me below the surface.

A crocodile had taken me, and I wanted to fight, but I couldn't even see it. "Please help me, God!" I tried to exclaim but to no avail as I was underwater, so instead, I swallowed a mouthful of the filthy river water.

A human's perception of time slows down when you are about to die. As I believed my days to be over, I saw all the happy times I had with my family and I regretted that my last encounter with my father had been a negative one. Why had I lost that fishing net and made my father angry? Why did we have to part on bad terms?

I came to peace with my mortality. I would soon meet with my family again in heaven, where all the small quarrels we had would be forgiven and we could live in an eternal pure bliss.

I came back to my senses as I saw the blue sky and the sun shining above me. Was this heaven? Then I saw Phillippe shouting at me, and I concluded that if I were dead, I had gone to hell. I passed out and everything turned black.

· · · ·

GASP *BARRF*

I woke up as I vomited up the filthy river water, which I had swallowed moments earlier. My lungs were in pain, as was my right arm. I looked up and I saw Phillippe sitting next to me.

"What happened?" I coughed.

"A small crocodile attacked you. I chopped it with my machete until it let go of you." Phillippe replied.

"What about the Interahamwe militia?" I asked.

"They were never coming. I just needed you to get in the water." Phillippe said.

"Why did I need to go first?" I asked.

"Because if I went first, no-one would have saved me if a crocodile attacked. This was the only way." Phillippe stated.

I didn't reply. Phillippe had used me as bait to find out if any crocodiles were nearby. While his recklessness had almost cost me my life, there was no point in arguing about it. We were finally in Tanzania, after walking for weeks through a war-torn Rwanda filled with deaths and horrors.

Phillippe grabbed my arm, studied the wound from the crocodile bite, and muttered. "Fucking hell, I need to deliver the girl untainted."

I looked at him and replied: "What are you talking about?"

Phillippe cleared his throat and replied: "The crocodile bite might be infected from the dirty water. We need to cauterize it."

"Cauterize?" I asked in confusion.

"Yes. I'll start a fire and heat my machete. As I put the hot machete on your wound, it will kill the bacteria inside it." Phillippe explained.

"But what about going to the hospital? We are safe here, right?" I asked.

Phillippe slapped me in an outburst of anger and exclaimed. "Stop questioning me, spoiled girl. The hospital won't treat a poor Rwandan fugitive. They would send you to the refugee camp and let your wound fester. I am the only reason you're alive. Do as I say!"

"I am sorry." I whimpered.

Phillippe muttered some indistinct curses and proceeded to start a fire. I stared in horror at the machete as the fire made the metal shimmer.

"Bite on this," Phillippe said and handed me a tree branch.

Arrp *Grunt* *Fizzz*

I bit the branch so hard to suppress my desire to kick Phillippe when he cauterized my wound with the glowing hot machete. After a while, the pain subsided, and I collapsed from the exhaustion.

Because of Phillippe's rudimentary way of dealing with my crocodile bite, I'll always have a large scar on my right arm. Yet, that scar is not the worst scar I bear from my months in Tanzania...

Chapter 6: The Garden of Eden before the snake; June 1994.

"We are here."

Phillippe looked relieved and happy as he uttered these words, and I saw him do something I couldn't recall seeing for over a month. I saw Phillippe smile. As he smiled, I perceived him as much younger than I had before, and I realised that he couldn't be much older than me. When he smiled, he looked like he was younger than 20.

I had grown quite fond of my captor who had beaten me repeatedly in the last month. I am not sure if this was Stockholm syndrome or because Phillippe, as bad as he was, was still better than the murderous thugs in the Interahamwe militia.

"What is this place?" I asked.

"This is the Nyakasanza residence of Mbwana Kapombe, the mining tycoon." Phillippe replied.

"I don't understand. Why are we here?" I asked.

Phillippe's breathing got louder, and I saw how his pupils dilated. This was his tell-tale sign that he would soon turn to violence. I froze and scolded myself. Why couldn't I keep my mouth shut? Phillippe calmed down. He forced a smile and replied.

"Mr Kapombe had a vision that he would find a suitable bride for his teenage son in the Gatsibo region of Rwanda. He sent me to find that bride, but then the civil war broke out. When I found you, I knew you were the one."

"Are you that son?" I asked.

Phillippe laughed and replied: "If I were that son, I wouldn't leave my palace to visit hell on earth. No, Samantha, I am a poor Hutu man who works for Mr Kapombe. In any case, our journey is over. Let's enter the mansion so I can get paid and you can find yourself a new home."

"But what if I don't want to marry his son?" I objected.

Phillippe stopped laughing. He gave me an ice-cold stare and spoke. "You will do as I say. As long as I deliver you to Mr Kapombe and get paid, I don't care what happens next. Yet, I will kill you if you give them any reason to not accept you into their household. Do we have an understanding?"

I nodded and didn't dare to say anything.

Phillippe muttered some curses, dragged me to the intercom, and called. As the intercom answered, Phillippe spoke:

"Halo. Ni Davide. Nilimleta msichana Bw Kapombe aliyeombwa."

Although I knew very little Swahili, I shivered when I realised that Phillippe wasn't his real name. Yet, I didn't want to press the issue or ask about the phone call.

The gate opened and two bodyguards and a maid came to greet us. After conversing with Phillippe in Swahili for a while, the maid approached me and spoke in English.

"Welcome to Mr Kapombe's mansion, Samantha. I am Mansa and I'll be your caretaker. Mr Kapombe is out of town, but he will be so glad to hear that the promised girl has arrived."

I smiled at Mansa, faked some enthusiasm, and replied. "I am happy to be here. I can't wait to meet Mr Kapombe's son."

. . . .

HEARING THIS, MANSA looked puzzled, but eventually, she shrugged it off and replied: "Oh yes. Mr Kapombe's son is out of town with his father but I am sure they'll return when they find out about your arrival. Now come with me. You need to bathe after your long trip and then I'll feed you our best foods to nurse you back to health."

"Thank you," I said and I followed Mansa as she led me to the bathroom and poured me a hot bath with bath foam.

I felt a sharp pain as my cauterized wound touched the hot water, but after a while, I relaxed. I felt excited by the prospect of a new life in wealth, far away from the horrors I had experienced. I closed my eyes and tried to picture my handsome future prince, but there was a foreboding feeling that I couldn't get out of my mind. I shook it off, and I focused on scrubbing the dirt off my body until the water was black from the dirt that my body had collected during over a month on the road.

. . . .

AS I FINISHED MY BATH, I put on the clean clothes that Mansa had left for me. It felt amazing to wear clean clothes for the first time in over a month. I thought about whether I should call for Mansa, but my curiosity took over and I left the bathroom and set out to look for her. I walked around in the mansion, and I was amazed at the luxury and the modern facility in the building. As I look back, Mbwana Kapombe's mansion wasn't that impressive, but I came from abject poverty, so I had a different perspective at the time.

As I came to an open door, I heard a conversation between Phillippe and Mansa. They were not aware of my presence, and they argued in my native language Kinyarwanda. I stopped behind the door to eavesdrop.

Phillippe:

- Stop saying that the girl is damaged. I want full payment for bringing her here.

Mansa:

- She has a large fresh wound on her right arm. How can I know that the rest of her body is of satisfactory standard for my master?

Phillippe:

- The girl is a virgin. I killed two men in Rwanda to make sure of it. She is the daughter of Mutara Nyamwasa, she is the girl your master hired me to fetch. Mr Kapombe can attest to it when he gets here.

Mansa:

- If that's the case, why can't you wait for my master to return?

Phillippe:

- Your master is very ill, and for all we know he might already be dead. This job was meant to be easy, but then the bloody civil war happened, which made it very difficult. I want my USD$50,000. I have other places to go.

Mansa:

- Okay. But if the girl won't be enough to cure our master, we are coming after you.

Phillippe:

- Well, she wouldn't be able to cure him. I already told your master that his idea wouldn't work, but he insisted on me getting him a virgin.

Mansa:

- Okay. Your money is in this bag. I need to look after the girl now.

Hearing this, I hurried back to the bathroom as I didn't want to let Mansa know that I had been eavesdropping on her conversation.

· · · ·

TIME PASSED AND I GRADUALLY felt more at home in the Kapombe Mansion. Mansa was a strict and distant caretaker, but at least she provided me with good food, clean clothes, and plenty of literature to still my thirst for knowledge. My main concern was loneliness, but my family was gone no matter what. Besides, from watching the television news, I knew that rape and disease were very prevalent in the United Nations-sponsored refugee camps in Tanzania.

I often speculated about the existence of Kapombe's mysterious son, who I was meant to marry. While the thought of forced marriage didn't appeal to me, it wasn't unheard of, and considering what I had been through, the thought didn't scare me. What did scare me was the realisation that Mbwana Kapombe didn't have a son. I came to this conclusion from checking a few of the photo albums he had in his bookcase. His son wasn't in any of the photos. It seemed unlikely that he would never include his son in his photographs since he had hired Phillippe to travel to Rwanda and kidnap a bride for his son.

I often recalled the conversation I had overheard between Phillippe and Mansa. Knowing that Phillippe had travelled to Rwanda to kidnap me changed everything. Our encounter wasn't by chance. Phillippe had travelled to my village to kidnap me, and he would have done so even if the genocide didn't take place. This changed my opinion about him. After I found out about this, I hated him for what he did to me. Although there was one man I would always hate the most, Patrick Bagosora.

Sometimes I speculated about the prophecy. What could it entail, and how would it affect my life? My gut-feeling told me that the prophecy wouldn't be good for me, but I wanted logic to govern my decision. If Mbwana hadn't sent Phillippe to kidnap me, I would be dead by now. The least I could do was to stay until Mbwana Kapombe arrived and thank him for saving me. Besides, my option to escape the mansion wasn't enticing. I could either decide to await my fate here in a golden cage, or I could await my destiny in the filthy and dangerous refugee camp. I chose to stay, which I thought was right at the time, but oh boy was I wrong...

Chapter 7: The Devil in Disguise; July 1994.

When I close my eyes, I never see visions of Mbwana Kapombe haunting me. In a way, it is strange, as what he did to me should have scarred me more than witnessing Patrick Bagosora murder my family. I guess my mind came to peace as I killed him when I left the Kapombe mansion.

I had lived at the Kapombe mansion for over a month when Mansa one day approached me and spoke. "Dress up in your nicest clothes, Samantha. Master Kapombe has finally returned."

I smiled, got dressed in a blue satin dress, and followed Mansa to the dining room of the mansion.

As I got to the dining room, I saw Mbwana Kapombe in person for the first time. He was a mere shadow of the portraits I had seen in the mansion. In front of me, I saw a sickly skinny man with ghoulish features accompanied by two body-guards. I knew from one look at him that Mr Kapombe was at death's door.

Mbwana smiled and walked towards me. "Oh, it really is you. The prophecy will come true. Thank God for Davide's loyalty and perseverance." Mbwana uttered weakly with tears in his eyes.

I looked at Mbwana with a dumbfounded expression on my face and asked. "What is the prophecy, and how do you know I am the one?"

Mbwana took out a photograph and showed it to me. I remembered when the photograph was taken. It had been a few years earlier. On the photograph, there was me, my father, and a man in a suit. Could that man be Mbwana? I looked at Mbwana and compared the two. The dissimilarities between the successful businessman on the photograph and the sickly man in front of me were many, but it was the same person.

"Is this photo of you with my father and I?" I asked.

"Yes. How would Davide otherwise find you?" Mbwana asked rhetorically.

"He told me his name was Phillippe." I replied.

"He used an alias. It is dangerous travelling into a war zone." Mbwana replied.

"So, why did he bring me here?" I asked.

Mbwana took a deep breath, looked around the room, and replied:

"Because of a prophecy. When I visited your village two years ago, I was in the prime of my life. I came across a witch that put a curse on me. Look at me now, I am dying. The divine mother in this village told me that finding a pure soul from the same village was the only way to lift the curse."

When I heard Mbwana's story, I recalled the fate of one of the villagers, Filonne. She had a similar disease to Mbwana and after she had died, public health officials came to my village and warned about a new disease called HIV.

"Was the witch's name Filonne?" I asked.

Mbwana looked at me in surprise and replied in indignation. "Yes, Filonne was her name. Cursed be that name for what she did to me."

I held my tongue. I didn't want to reveal that Filonne had died a year earlier from the same disease Mbwana had. Some truths are better left unsaid, particularly when you meet a person for the first time.

"Please, Mr Kapombe. Let's say grace and have some chicken soup. I am sure the prophecy will come true now that you and Samantha are living under the same roof." Mansa said and served us the chicken soup at the dining table.

When I drank the soup, I reflected that the soup tasted a bit odd. I kept eating though, as I didn't want to appear rude and picky in front of my host and benefactor. As I finished the soup, I felt dizzy, collapsed to the floor, and passed out.

. . . .

AS I WOKE UP, I FOUND myself buck naked, facing down into the bed with my arms and legs spread apart and tied to the bed frame. I heard Mbwana panting. He showed his erect penis in front of my eyes and spoke. "That fucking bitch, Filonne. She let me fuck her so she could pass on her curse to me. Now I am dying and the only way to save myself is to fuck your virgin pussy."

I felt terrified and helpless. I wasn't just about to be raped; a man with a terrifying disease was about to rape me. I sobbed and tried to reason with Mbwana. "Mr Kapombe. Please. It doesn't work that way. Filonne died from her disease last year. You won't save yourself by raping me. You'll doom us both."

Mbwana slapped me and shouted. "Shut up. That's what my stupid doctor said. But he can't cure me, can he? I must save myself."

Having said this, Mbwana walked behind me and forced his manhood upon me while he pushed my face down the mattress to muffle my cries. I experienced excruciating pain as he entered me, and time slowed down. Although the rape sequence only lasted a few minutes, it felt like a hell loop having the disease-stricken man force himself upon me.

As Mbwana finished his dirty deed, he left me strung up in the bed. I assume this was to increase my pain from lying in the awkward position while my vagina was bleeding from the blunt trauma. I lay like this for hours, sobbing and wishing for death until Mansa entered my room and untied me. She left without a word and locked the door behind her.

• • • •

I WAS IN THE BATH SCRUBBING myself frantically to get rid of the stench and sickness from my body. It was all in vain. No matter how hard I scrubbed, I couldn't rid myself of the disgust I felt thinking about Mbwana's terrible touch and HIV-infected spunk. I noticed how the bathwater turned red from the blood coming out of my vagina. In my shocked state, I had scrubbed myself so hard, so my genitals were bleeding.

"OOOOOYYYAAAA!"

I let out an anguished scream that alerted Mansa, and she entered my bathroom. She stared at me and the blood-soaked bathwater in terror and exclaimed. "Samantha, what are you doing?"

"He raped me, and I can't get this disgusting feeling out of my head." I sobbed uncontrollably.

Mansa shook her head and replied. "Mbwana is back in the hospital. He didn't scrub your body until it was bleeding, you did."

"But I must get him out of my head." I wailed.

"Then fight him in your head, little darling. You are a strong girl, Samantha. I can see it in your eyes. Don't do this to yourself." Mansa urged.

I nodded and sobbed in silence. Mansa was right. I hadn't survived the Rwandan genocide to be driven to insanity and suicide by a sick twisted man. I would survive, and I would make sure that I told everyone my story. Why else had I survived the attack on my village that killed the rest of my family?

Mansa got down on her knees and hugged me while I was in the bathtub. I reciprocated her hug. While a part of me hated her for working for Mbwana, I also needed a friend to give me comfort. I could not face all the horrors of the world alone as humans are meant to face obstacles together. After the hug, Mansa looked after my wounds and she spent the rest of the day braiding my hair. This was the closest I had felt to someone since the day Patrick Bagosora murdered my family and I lost my dear mother.

• • • •

I GUESS I SHOULD HAVE left the Kapombe Mansion when Mr Kapombe was in the hospital. If I had left, I wouldn't have sustained life-altering injuries. So why did I stay? I guess it was because I had connected with Mansa and because we were convinced that Mbwana Kapombe would never come back from the hospital. If that prediction were correct, it wouldn't make sense to abandon the safety of the mansion to live in a crowded and filthy refugee camp.

During Mbwana's absence, hope started returning to my life. The Rwandan Patriotic Front had ousted the Interahamwe militia from Rwanda and the civil war and mass-killings had finally ended. I prayed to Jesus Christ every night that some of my kin had survived, and I would be able to return to my village and rebuild what little we had left, after what the reckless hatred had destroyed.

One day, a bowl of foul-tasting chicken soup quashed all my hopes...

Chapter 8: Killing the devil; August 1994.

"You filthy whore! The prophecy didn't come true. You fucked someone else before me!"

The room was still spinning from the sedatives in my soup when I woke up to find myself naked and tied to the bed. As for orientation, the major difference was that I was lying on my back and faced the ceiling instead of facing the mattress.

As my vision got clearer, I noticed that Mbwana was fully clothed. This filled me with terror. I would rather face the evil I knew, over the evil I didn't know.

"Are you going to rape me again?" I slurred.

"No. What's the point? You deceived me. You weren't a virgin, and I couldn't lift the curse. Now I have only a few weeks left to live, and it is too late for me to find a girl to lift my curse." Mbwana revealed.

"I was a virgin; you saw the blood." I sobbed.

"That doesn't matter. The curse was not lifted. Someone else fucked you before I did. Was it Davide?" Mbwana accused. I shook my head.

Mbwana punched me in the gut and shouted: "Don't lie to me, Samantha."

"I am not lying, you sick fuck." I shouted.

I regretted those words as I saw how Mbwana's gaze blackened. "You did fuck someone. I am sure you liked it too, you dirty slut. You weren't pleading and whining when Davide entered you, did you?" Mbwana taunted.

I spat Mbwana in the face, and he smiled a sadistic smile towards me. "You'll regret that, Samantha."

"What do you want from me? Do you expect me to beg for my life? Just kill me and get it over with." I defied in stride.

Mbwana shook his head, smiled, and spoke. "I am not going to kill you. I will take the joy of sex away from you. Since you doomed me by fucking someone else before we met, that will be my parting gift."

I stared in horror as Mbwana picked up a knife and a large baton from his duffle bag on the floor. I screamed and twisted my frail body in extreme suffering and pain when he started cutting my clitoris with deliberate slow cuts. Mbwana sneered wickedly at me, as he held up my severed lady parts and dangled them in front of his face like a sick taunt. As I saw him with my blood and dismembered clitoris in front of my face, I saw the devil's face and I knew I needed to kill him, even if it were the last thing I would ever do.

Mbwana chucked away my cut-off clitoris and smirked. "I have destroyed you on the outside, now I will destroy you on the inside."

After saying this, he pulled out a large baton and forced it into my vagina. I screamed in unspeakable pain until I went into shock from the torture and passed out.

* * * * *

"MR KAPOMBE IS SLEEPING on his bed. His door is unlocked."

I opened my eyes very slowly and I saw the blurry face of Nassor, who was one of Mbwana's bodyguards. After untying me, the man left without a word.

I tried to get up to a seated position. The immense pain that stretched from my vagina to my stomach all the way to my face made it almost impossible to get up, but I would not die here. I needed to kill Mbwana for what he did to me. I got up and I tried to stop the bleeding by applying a white T-shirt to my wounds. It didn't seem to help as my T-shirt was soaked with fresh blood.

"I must kill the devil." I mumbled dazedly as I picked up the knife and the baton that Mbwana had left on the floor with all my might. I gathered my mental strength and dragged myself to the room where Mbwana was sleeping.

As I got to Mbwana's room, I felt a surge of powerful energy I have never felt before, a feeling that I had suppressed all these time from all the hatred and fury. While he was still sleeping, I swung the baton in his head repetitively, as hard as I can, blow after blow, till his face and nose was broken and his tooth had fallen out. After that, I stabbed him multiple times in the chest until his raspy breaths got weaker and finally ended.

I dragged myself to a chair, got seated, closed my eyes, and waited for myself to slowly bleed out to my merciful death. As I faded into unconsciousness, I felt a sense of satisfaction that I had killed my rapist and tormentor. Amidst all the pain and disorientation, I remembered that I must stay alive in order to avenge my family and my people from the malevolent Patrick Bagosora.

* * * *

I GOT BACK TO MY SENSES when I heard how Mansa was cooking break-fast in the kitchen. She would serve her master breakfast in his room, and she would find him dead from multiple stabbing wounds and with his face crushed. It was better if I wasn't in the room when this happened. I thought of coming clean to the Tanzanian authorities and tell them what had happened, but I was afraid. I was a poor Tutsi refugee that had murdered a wealthy Tanzanian man in his sleep. Would they believe me if I told them about how he raped and mutilated me, or would they claim that my wounds were self-inflicted?

I didn't want to find out, so I opened the window, mustered my strength, and climbed out. The United Nations refugee camp was only a few kilometres away. Despite my mistrust for the UN, I would rather take my chances with them than staying here and deal with the local police. As I got down on the road, I heard a loud scream followed by ruckus from the Kapombe Mansion. Mansa had found Mbwana's corpse, and I could only pray that I would get to the UN refugee camp before the police got to me...

Chapter 9: Delirious in the UN refugee camp; August 1994.

Several hours later, I arrived at the United Nations refugee camp. The camp was only a few kilometres away from the Kapombe Mansion, but it had been the hardest journey of my life. The pain from my mutilated genitalia, combined with the loss of blood had made me very weak, and I had collapsed several times on the way. The worst part, however, was my fear and paranoia. The only thing that kept me going was the thought that I have to survive.

I was a poor Tutsi refugee who had murdered a Tanzanian business tycoon in his sleep. The police would never believe me if I tell them that he raped and mutilated me. Worse yet, I feared that a mob would come to kill me like I had seen mobs do to others during the Rwandan genocide. As I approached the refugee camp, two soldiers with blue helmets approached me. One of them shouted:

"This camp is full. Return to Rwanda. The war is over."

I struggled to stand up and give the soldier a coherent response. There was nothing I wanted more than returning to my village and pretend like these terrible months hadn't happened. However, there was an issue. Mbwana had mutilated my genitalia, and I was likely to die from infection if I didn't get medical treatment.

"Please help me..." I wheezed.

"Are you deaf? This camp is full. Go somewhere else." The soldier shouted.

I didn't respond. The combination of blood-loss, exhaustion, and dehydration caused me to collapse to the ground. I reached a delirious state where I saw Jesus and the Devil Lucifer argued about the fate of my soul.

"Let her come with me to my Father's house. She is an innocent child." Jesus said.

"She murdered a man in cold blood. She will murder again. Her soul is mine." The Devil Lucifer replied.

"It doesn't matter. She is welcome to my Father's kingdom if she repents her sins." Jesus stated.

I reflected over Jesus's words. I couldn't ask him for forgiveness for murdering Mbwana Kapombe. To ask for forgiveness, I had to feel sorry for what I had done, but I wasn't. Mbwana was a monster, and he had mutilated me. If I hadn't sought vengeance, then who would have avenged me and brought him to justice?

"I am coming with you, Lucifer". I mumbled, and as I closed my eyes, I heard his evil laughter in my head. As I slowly opened my eyes again, I saw a beautiful guardian angel in the form of a blond female doctor with warm blue eyes, looking at me deeply with love and care.

"Her genitalia have been mutilated. We need to give her medical treatment straight away." The white female doctor said to someone, and I was carried and floated gently towards a medical tent on a stretcher. Once I was in the hospital camp, I landed on a warm and clean bed, and I continued listening to Jesus Christ and the Devil Lucifer arguing about my soul until I passed out.

• • • •

AS I WOKE UP, I FELT a searing thirst that drove me to scream for water. "Water. Please I need water."

A nurse in blood-covered scrubs handed me a cup before she returned to the patient next to me. I sculled the water, but I shouldn't have, as the sudden hydration put my body into shock, and I vomited it all out again. I looked around in shock at the room I was in. Injured and dying people were seen everywhere in this filthy hospital camp. I noticed how the nurses struggled to stop the bleeding of a man who had his legs blown off by a landmine. Had I survived my condition, or had I come to arrive in hell? My inability to still my searing thirst indicated that I had arrived in hell. "Please Jesus help me. I am sorry I didn't seek your forgiveness." I sobbed.

"I'll look after this patient." A female doctor shouted. As she approached me, I recognised her as the doctor that had saved me the previous day.

The doctor spoke to me gently, "You need to drink in small sips, my dear. Your body needs time to absorb liquid after your surgery.

"Will I be okay?" I wept.

"Yes, you'll be okay." The doctor soothed.

The doctor helped me sitting upright, while I took a few sips of the water. As I finished sipping my cup of water, she smiled at me and spoke: "Good girl. Slow and steady wins the race."

I nodded, closed my eyes, and fell asleep.

Chapter 10: In trouble with the law; September 1994.

Sometimes, good intentions can have bad outcomes. I am sure that Dr Amy Schofield didn't have bad intentions when she contacted the police, yet it almost cost me my life. If I had been upfront to her about what had happened, she might have acted differently. In the end, it didn't matter as Jesus still watched over me.

It all started a few days after my surgery. I was in pain, and my paranoia tormented me. The United Nations refugee camp attendants had given me a tent to sleep in, but I didn't feel safe in it. I was alone, and I feared that some of the other refugees would come in at night and rape me. I was even more terrified that the police would come after me for what I did to Mbwana Kapombe.

The blonde female doctor who had saved me visited me in my tent.

"So, how are you feeling now?" The doctor asked gently.

"Not too good. I need to leave this depressing place. I hope I can get in contact with my relatives. I want to go back to my village." I replied weakly.

"I see. What's your last name? We have people working at reuniting families." The doctor replied.

I hesitated. I felt terrified about what would happen if I gave the authorities my full name. Mbwana Kapombe had asked Phillippe to kidnap me for a reason, and everyone in the Kapombe Mansion knew my full name. Chances were that the police were already looking for me concerning Mbwana's murder.

"I don't want to give you my full name. I am afraid that bad men are looking for me." I whispered. "The bad men that raped and mutilated you?" The female doctor asked.

"Yes..." I started to cry.

The doctor hugged me, kissed my forehead, and tried to comfort me. "It's okay, love. I can protect you."

"I don't even know your name." I said softly.

"My name is Amy Schofield, and I am from Australia," Amy revealed with a strong and confident voice.

"Okay. I will be truthful. My last name is Nyamwasa. Please find my relatives. I just want to go home." I pleaded.

"I promise I'll do everything I can," Amy assured.

I nodded and tried my best to give her a smile, as the beautiful and gentle Amy wiped my tears with a handkerchief. After a few minutes of silence, Amy spoke again. "Would you like to tell me who raped you? Perhaps we can punish them for what they did."

I have often reflected over what would have happened if I came clean with Amy at this moment. Would she have contacted the police if I told her that I killed Mbwana Kapombe after he raped me, or would she have understood and kept silent? I didn't reply at that time, which was a foolish choice, since she already knew my full name, and she had promised to look for my relatives.

• • • •

"SAMANTHA NYAMWASA? I am Detective Pesa Nassoro from the Tanzanian Police. Do you mind if I come in?"

I froze and stared in terror at the burly man who stood in the opening of my small tent. I had seen many men like him slaughter and torture my peers over the last few months. Most of all, I feared his reason for visiting.

Pesa didn't wait for my reply. He entered my tent and squatted next to me. He pulled out a photograph from his pocket and threw it at me. I looked at the photo. It was a crime scene photo of how the cops found Mbwana Kapombe, after I bludgeoned him to death.

"Do you know why I am here?" Pesa accused.

As I shook my head, Pesa slapped me.

"Don't lie to me, Samantha," Pesa shouted.

"I am sorry..." I whispered.

"I can't hear you," Pesa exclaimed.

"I am sorry!" I yelled.

Pesa nodded and studied me in silence for a while. After a piercing silence that shook me to the core with fear, he spoke again. "So, let me be clear. If you ever lie to me again, I'll lock you up and throw away the key. Do we understand each other?"

I nodded.

"So why did you kill Mbwana Kapombe? He gave you refuge and a nice place to stay. Yet you murdered him in his sleep." Pesa continued with his intimidations.

"He raped me. He tortured and mutilated me." I said in defiance.

Pesa punched me in the face and broke my nose. "I told you not to lie to me, Tutsi vermin. Mr Kapombe's housekeeper, Mansa, told me you were a deluded girl who turned to self-harm and cut your own genitalia. You murdered the man who protected you. That's how crazy you are." Pesa ranted.

"I am telling you the truth. He tortured and mutilated me." I wheezed in defiance.

Pesa kicked me in the gut and sent my body into shock. Blood was flowing out from my genitalia, as the kick opened the wounds that Mbwana had caused a week earlier. Pesa dragged me from the ground to an upright position. He stared into my eyes and hissed. "You killed a great man from my village. Admit your crimes and the people will judge you fairly. Lie and you shall suffer."

"What on earth is going on in here?"

Pesa pushed me to the ground and turned to the source of the voice, Dr Amy Schofield.

"This girl is a killer. I am bringing her with me." Pesa shouted.

"You are doing no such thing. You came here to ask her a few questions, not to beat her into a pulp." Amy replied sternly.

"You can't tell me what to do. This is my country." Pesa warned.

"You are in a United Nations refugee camp. This area is under UN jurisdiction." Amy stated.

Pesa was about to attack Amy when two UN soldiers entered the tent. "Dr Schofield. What is going on?" One of the soldiers asked.

"This man is trespassing. Please escort him away from the camp." Amy commanded.

Pesa gazed at Amy with hateful eyes, as he left the UN camp without further confrontation.

· · · ·

"WHY DIDN'T YOU TELL me the truth that you killed Mbwana Kapombe?" Amy asked me.

"I was afraid. Look what happened." I sobbed.

"It wouldn't have happened if you told me the truth," Amy stated.

"I am sorry. I should have trusted you." I whimpered.

Amy sat silent for a while. She looked away in the distance, and she seemed to be reflecting over her choices. Eventually, she spoke.

"We need to leave Tanzania straight away. It's not ideal, but I fear what will happen if Pesa returns with a mob to attack us. The locals admired Mbwana for his efforts to develop the Nyakasanza region."

"So, you'll risk your life to save me?" I asked.

"I didn't come to Africa to let the innocent suffer," Amy replied strongly.

"I am not innocent. I did kill him." I objected.

"You cannot get a fair trial here. Mbwana had it coming for what he did to you." Amy stated.

"Thank you, Amy." I whispered.

Amy muttered something, grabbed a large blanket, and spoke. "Come with me. We are leaving."

I followed Amy to her car, and I hid in the trunk of the car while Amy drove us to Burundi, away from the dangers we faced in Tanzania.

Chapter 11: Leaving for Australia; October 1994.

We were eating Boko Boko hares, which is a Burundian chicken stew, and watching the sunset over Lake Tanganyika when Amy spoke to me. "I have some good news and some bad news."

I looked at her in anticipation. The last few weeks had been peaceful, and we had connected, although I hadn't been able to enjoy the feeling of being free. Nightmares had tormented me, and I felt terrified every time I saw a police officer. To me, the men in uniform were all the same, and although the Burundi police force had left me alone this far, I feared that I would soon come across another Pesa or Phillippe that would torment and rape me.

Amy spoke again:

"The good news is that I have secured you a refugee visa to Australia. My cousin has a nice house in the countryside there. She can look after you, and give you a good upbringing."

I reflected on Amy's statement. I didn't know much about Australia, except for it being a very faraway country, with mostly white people living in it.

"But I don't want to go to Australia. I want things to go back to as they were." I sobbed.

"I understand, but it is safer for you to live in Australia until Rwanda has healed as a country. Moving to Australia won't take your heritage away from you." Amy explained kindly.

"Okay. I guess you're right. Thank you, Amy." I replied after a while.

I hugged Amy as the sun set at the horizon of the lake. I forced a smile and spoke, "So, when are we going to Australia?"

"I have booked a flight for you on Wednesday. I need to return to Tanzania. I have filed a complaint against Pesa Nassoro to the central government of Tanzania in Dar-Es-Salaam. They are seeing me on Thursday." Amy revealed.

"No, don't go. It's too dangerous. What if they arrest you?" I objected.

"They won't, and besides, I need to stand up for the little people like yourself," Amy replied.

I didn't say anything. While I was upset that Amy would risk her life, I couldn't argue against it. Her willingness to risk her well-being for others was the reason I was still alive. Yet, I felt very sad that our paths would diverge. Amy was a good person and the closest I had felt to love and connection since the horrible events that took everything away from me and scarred my body and mind.

"I will pray to Jesus to keep you safe," I said and hugged Amy as the last rays of sunlight blessed us with its lifegiving energy.

* * * *

I FELT A MIXTURE OF anticipation and melancholic excitement as the plane took off from Bujumbura Airport. I had never been on an aeroplane, and if someone had told me that I would be flying this year, I would have laughed at their silliness. Yet, there was nothing for me to laugh about now. As sad as I was to leave my country behind, there was nothing that bound me to Rwanda anymore. My family was dead, and as far as I knew, that applied to my other relatives as well.

I looked at the flight tickets that would take me to Australia. I would need to swap flights twice before I landed at Adelaide International Airport. I felt anxious at the task at hand. What if I lost my tickets along the way, or couldn't navigate to the right airport terminal? Amy had told me that some airports were huge, like the size of a whole city, and it would be easy to get lost in such a foreign place.

I shook off my worries. I had survived the Rwandan genocide, Phillippe's unpredictable temper swings, Mbwana Kapombe's torture and humiliation, and Pesa Nassoro's violent interrogation tactics. I would survive this trip to Australia, where my new life could begin.

Having calmed myself down, I started reading the books about Australia that Amy gave me. The rest of my life was ahead of me, and I wanted to start my new life running fresh.

Chapter 12: Years of sorrow, January 1995.

It is hard loving someone if you see them as a substitute for a lost one, instead of a unique individual. My adoptive mother Lisa Henshaw and I would had better lives together, if we had appreciated our individual uniqueness instead of seeing each other as mere replacements.

Lisa had called herself black, and blamed racism for the death of her daughter. To me, her statement didn't make any sense as I saw her as white with a tiny bit more melanin than your average white person. Yet, she claimed to be a proud aboriginal woman and blamed The Stolen Generations for all her problems. I guess to an outsider, the distinction between Hutus and Tutsis is equally nonsensical. Humans tend to argue about distinctions without a difference, and often these nonsensical dogmas drive our species to insanity.

Lisa's daughter Daphne had died six months before my arrival in Australia. She had died by her own hand. The bullying she experienced in school from being the only aboriginal child in the town had pushed her over the edge. She had taken her mother's painkillers and swallowed the whole lot of them, which caused her to overdose and die. I knew that as much as Lisa tried projecting the anger and blame onto others, she blamed herself the most for what had happened. It was her drugs that had killed her daughter.

Lisa often called me Daphne when she was drunk, or off her head on prescription pills. The notion was absurd as we didn't look at all alike, but I guess it was a function of how Lisa perceived me as a replacement for her lost daughter.

As for me, I saw Lisa as a desperate replacement of comfort from the beautiful and gentle Amy who had saved and took care of me. While Amy was energetic, intelligent, and committed to making the world a better place, Lisa was her opposite. Lisa saw herself as a victim of circumstances, and instead of building a better life for us, she chose to get drunk and blame her misery on others. As time passed, I grew resentful towards Lisa, and things got worse when I heard about Amy's death.

. . . .

OUR CHOICES IN LIFE can have a ripple effect that affects all future outcomes. I don't know whether it was my fault that Amy died in Tanzania, if it was a consequence of her idealistic personality, or if it was just a pure coincidence. What I do know is that Amy's death affected me severely, and crushed my spirit to pieces.

As I came home from school one day, I noticed Lisa was drunker than usual. This surprised me, as Lisa usually looked after the farm and the animals during the day, and the heavy drinking was her night-time only activity.

"She is dead. This is your fault." Lisa slurred.

I prepared myself for a confrontation. I didn't accept to be other people's punching bags. Lisa's choice to adopt me didn't give her the right to abuse me. "For the last time. I am not Daphne, and it is not my fault that she killed herself." I shouted and I was about to leave and slam the door behind me when Lisa stunned me with her revelation. "Amy is dead. The authorities found her body close to the Nyakasanza refugee camp."

. . . .

HEARING THIS, MY WORLD fell apart. I had been counting the days, hoping that Amy would come back to Australia and take me away from this shithole. Amy couldn't have intended for me to be abused by her drunken cousin. If she had come back to Australia, she would have taken me in and formed me to a better person. If Amy was dead, there was no-one left in my world to care about anymore, and there was nothing left to live for.

Realising that Amy wouldn't come for me, I had to reach out to my drunken custodian.

"I am so sorry to hear that. Amy saved my life." I exclaimed and approached Lisa to give her a hug.

She pushed me aside and shouted. "Don't touch me, you filthy nigger. This is all your fault."

Hearing this from the vile hypocrite who always spoke about how racism made her life miserable, I snapped. I shoved her into the wall and rushed to the barn to spend the night with our farm animals. The animals were a better company than the mean drunk who was supposed to be my "mother".

. . . .

REFLECTING ON MY YEARS in the South Australian village of Wudinna, the racism was never a major issue to me. I don't know if my experience were different to Daphne's, but the small incidents that occurred would never had driven me to suicide. People have different mental strengths, and my mental strength made me become unaffected by minor issues such as name calling or teasing. I had survived too much to let a few inbred broods affect my life with their cruel words.

The relationship with my foster mother Lisa remained strained for the five years I lived in Wudinna. While we stayed out of each other's way, there was no love between us. Words can't describe the relief I felt when I turned 18 so I could finally move to Adelaide.

Lisa died a few months after I moved to Adelaide. A combination of severe drugs and alcohol addiction claimed her life, and she passed away at the young age of 42. I guess she had lost the remnants of her will to live when she no longer had to look after me. At times, I am blaming myself for not doing more to save Lisa from her own demons. But then I remember that I came to Lisa as a broken girl, ravaged from war and scarred of rape and genital mutilation. What person, except for Jesus, could help someone else under such circumstances?

Chapter 13: The end of my line; July 2016.

I was walking around in the world of dark shadow that once was my village in Rwanda. Everyone was dead and I heard haunting demonic laughters that tormented my mind. I felt the excruciating pain I experienced when Mbwana Kapombe mutilated my genitals coming back to haunt me.

I wanted to stay down and not move anywhere, but I wasn't in control, I knew where the dream would take me. I saw myself chopping Mbwana with a butcher's knife. As I stared into his lifeless eyes, maggots came crawling out of them. I flinched and jumped backwards from the decomposing body, and I was drawn to the sadistic laughter of Patrick Bagosora.

"I don't want to go. Please!" My younger self pleaded, but she was powerless to stop seeing what fate wanted her to see. My chest got heavy, and my breathing was staggered. I was suffocating, and yet I couldn't die and find peace. I walked to the hut I grew up in. I relived the horror from that fateful night. The soldiers chopped my father with their machetes and fired their arrows at my brother. Finally, I came across Patrick Bagosora who was raping and mutilating my mother. He slit her throat and stared at me with his demonic eyes. His gaze etched into my mind and made him impossible to forget. "You could have saved me." My mother chanted with a haunting voice, and I screamed in terror as a woke up in an extreme fright.

"Did you have the same dream again?" My husband Jakob said as he got up from our bed and wiped my sweat away with a nice warm towel.

"Yes, Jakob." I whimpered.

"I understand," Jakob said and held my hand lovingly.

I smiled. Jakob was the only thing that kept me grounded and stopped me from going insane. Yet our relationship was anything but normal, and I feared that my recurring nightmares from the past were because I couldn't see a future with him. I guess the reason was the circumstances around our marriage.

When I was in my 20's, I tried dating a few men. It always ended the same way, with me screaming in agonizing pain as we tried to have sex. Mbwana Kapombe did get the last laugh when he mutilated my genitals after his superstitious rape prophecy didn't cure him of his AIDS.

Although I was fortunate enough to not have caught HIV from my evil tormentor, I was incapable of having sex. I lost hope in the future, and I feared that I would walk the earth alone until the end of my days. Then one day, I met with Jakob when I started a new job in Adelaide. We became close, and the best part was that he didn't seem to have any sexual interest in me.

One night when we were having drinks, Jakob revealed to me that he felt terrified whenever he visited his family in Uganda. Jakob was a homosexual, and he feared that his family would find out. Homosexuality carried a lifetime prison term in Uganda, and it was common to murder homosexuals for the shame they brought to their family. This revelation affected me deeply, particularly since the bigots oppressed the homosexuals under the banner of Christianity, the same deity, who I have always kept close to my heart.

I had thought about Jakob's predicament and I had realised that destiny wanted us to meet. I couldn't have sex with men because of my genital mutilation, and Jakob had no interest in women sexually because of his homosexuality, but he wanted to get married to a woman. Our marriage was made with a lie, but it would be a lie that was good for both us and made us happy. Having this realisation, I had proposed to Jakob and he had agreed to marry me.

• • • •

WELL, I HAD BEEN WRONG. Marrying Jakob hadn't brought me happiness, it had merely brought me less sorrow. During our marriage, we only had sex once, on our wedding night, as Jakob wanted to try his best to consummate the marriage. It was a painful experience and I had settled for a lie, and I had no future to look forward to. Because of this, my obsession with the past had gotten worse.

"We can still have a future together," I mumbled to myself as I closed my eyes and fell asleep before the important day to come.

• • • •

I GUESS MY INFERTILITY shouldn't have come as a surprise, but I didn't know before we visited the IVF-clinic. In retrospect, I must have known all along, but I guess that denial is a powerful force of the human psyche.

Jakob and I had agreed to try to have children. It was my idea as I needed something to live for, and I hoped that having children of my own could be that something. I don't know whether it would have worked, but I guess I wouldn't obsess about tracking down Patrick Bagosora if I had the future of a child in my hands.

Meeting with Jane, the IVF-consultant, was quite awkward. Particularly, when we answered the question of how often we had sex. I answered. "A couple of times a week, depending on when the lust comes." Jakob wouldn't play along with this often-rehearsed lie and replied, "We don't have sex. That's why we are here."

Jane gave us a confused look. I cleared my throat and spoke: "Uhm, my husband is correct. We haven't had sex since our wedding night five years ago."

Jane blustered and said, "Uhm, are you sure that our IVF-clinic is the right place to visit? Normally people come here when they can't conceive, not because they don't want to have sex with their partner.

"Mbega ikiragi. Ntabwo agurisha neza ibicuruzwa bye. (What a dumb bitch. She is not exactly selling her product.)" I said to Jakob.

"Ba mwiza, Samantha. Ntabwo ari amakosa ye dufite ibihe bidasanzwe. (Be nice, Samantha. It's not her fault we have special circumstances.)" Jakob replied.

I cleared my throat and spoke: "We don't have sex because I was raped and mutilated when I was 12. Furthermore, Jakob is a homosexual who agreed to marry me because he fears what his family will do if they find out about his orientation."

Jane stared at us in disbelief for a while. She had no idea what to say. Eventually, she spoke. "I am sorry to hear about your childhood, Samantha. Have you visited a gynaecologist about your injuries? I think that would be preferable before we offer you fertility treatments."

I reflected on Jane's question. I hadn't visited a gynaecologist or sought any help for my physical or mental injuries. The last time I spoke to a doctor about what had happened to me, I got beaten up and my friend Amy died. I didn't want the past to come back to haunt me. However, if I didn't seek help, I wouldn't be able to have a future.

"Thanks for telling me, Jane. I want to book a gynaecologist session if that is what you recommend." I said.

"Of course. Please see Dr Michaela Baker. I'll write you a referral." Jane replied.

The meeting at the IVF-clinic lasted for another 15 minutes where we dealt with common questions and answers. After that, we went home.

· · · ·

I FELT A SURGE OF HATRED raging through me as I listened to what the doctor said. I hated that doctor Michaela Baker almost as much as I hated Patrick Bagosora. She had told me what I had feared all along but tried so hard to ignore. The damages done to my genitalia were too severe, and I would never be able to bear children. My family line died with me. Michaela Baker had killed my last glimmer of hope, and I wanted to find a target for my anger and hatred.

Rationally, I knew that Michaela hadn't done me anything. She wasn't the one who mutilated me, Mbwana Kapombe was the man I should have murderous thoughts about. But Michaela was the one who had killed my hope. This was something Mbwana had never achieved, and besides, I had killed him when I escaped the Kapombe Mansion.

"I hate her! I hate that bitch Michaela Baker!" I exclaimed to Jakob as I started smashing crockery in the kitchen.

Jakob gave me a worried look, but he didn't dare to approach me until my anger outburst had receded. A few minutes later, he approached me as I was sobbing in the kitchen, surrounded by broken glass and plates. He squatted next to me and lifted me to the bedroom, while whispering calming words.

As we reached our bedroom, Jakob spoke: "Why do you hate her? What did she do to you?"

"She ended my line. She told me I will never be able to bear children." I sobbed.

"You can't hate her for that. She is only the messenger." Jakob objected gently.

"I know. Yet it was her, not Patrick nor Mbwana, that killed my hope for the future." I replied.

"I guess we can always adopt a child?" Jakob suggested.

"Yes, I guess so," I said emotionlessly.

I know that Jakob's suggestion about adoption made sense, but at the time it was nothing that appealed to me. My line would die with me even if I adopted a child. Besides, I was wary of adoption considering the cold relationship I had with my adoptive mother Lisa. If I ever were to adopt a child, I couldn't see the child as a replacement for the child I never had. Loving a replacement didn't work.

Since I didn't feel ready to adopt a child, I delved into another project. I needed to find Patrick Bagosora and bring him to justice.

Chapter 14: Finding a lead on Patrick Bagosora; September 2016.

Sometimes our enemies are a lot closer to us than we imagine. When I started looking for Patrick Bagosora, I would not have anticipated that I would find him in Adelaide where I lived.

I had been searching for Patrick on Internet forums for months, when I received a video chat request. I was wary of scammers on these internet forums, but I couldn't let go of my chance to find out about Patrick's whereabouts. I felt shocked when I saw the video caller's name on the screen. It was Phillippe. Although he looked old and weathered, I was certain of it. He had the same facial features as the man who took me out of Rwanda, and he also had the same scar under his left eye.

When I saw Phillippe, mixed feelings of rage and thankfulness fucked up my mind. I was thankful that Phillippe had saved me from Patrick Bagosora and the Rwandan genocide, but I was also raging. The only reason Phillippe saved me was to sell me to a sadistic rapist, and he would have kidnapped me even if the Rwandan genocide never took place.

Phillippe spoke, "Samantha. It is so good to see you alive. I have been praying for you."

"I would have been safer if you didn't deliver me to a sadistic rapist." I shouted.

"I know. But God is punishing me. I won't live much longer." Phillippe revealed.

"Let me guess. You caught AIDS and raping a virgin didn't save you either?" I sniped sarcastically.

"I caught AIDS, but I would never rape a virgin." Phillippe replied.

"Wow, you must be man of the year then. Do you want an award?" I continued to mock.

"This was a mistake. I'm signing off." Phillippe said.

"Hold on. Stay on the line. I am sorry. Tell me what you wanted to say." I pretended to apologise, as I wanted to know what his true intentions were.

"You have been looking for Patrick Bagosora. I know his fake identity and location." Phillippe revealed.

"And you are sharing this with me because of the goodness of your heart?" I taunted distrustfully.

"I need money for medicine. I am dying." Phillippe pleaded.

"You should have saved some of the money you made from selling me. Once a con, always a con." I exclaimed, and then turned off the video chat with Phillippe as I couldn't bear to see his disgusting face any longer.

I took a deep breath, and I was shaking with rage. As much as I wanted to find Patrick Bagosora, I wouldn't pay that bastard Phillippe a cent to know his whereabouts. Chances were that Phillippe would defraud me, and I wouldn't get any closer to finding Patrick.

Phillipe video called me again. I hesitated, but I picked up the call. "The man you are looking for calls himself Laurence Juma. He is running an import/export company in Adelaide not far away from you. I am sorry for the pain I caused you, Samantha."

Having said this, Phillippe pulled up a pistol and shot himself in the head.

I stared in shock and disbelief at the screen. What had I just witnessed? Had Phillippe killed himself, or was this some kind of sick game? I realised that it would be easy to stage a suicide in front of a webcam, so I thought he must have faked it. I understood that there was no way for me to find out the truth at this stage, and besides it didn't matter to me. I did know one thing; however, Phillippe had given me a name, Laurence Juma, and that man supposedly lived in the same city as I, Adelaide.

Laurence Juma. I mumbled the name to myself a few times. If this man was Patrick Bagosora, I would find him in no time, and I would confront him for his crimes.

Chapter 15: Meeting with Patrick Bagosora; September 2016.

I was outside the Adelaide office of the Star of Africa corporation. Officially, the company was selling fair-trade coffee and cocoa beans, and various other food products. I suspected however, that this was a front for smuggling blood diamonds and other conflict resources to Australia.

I wasn't here to confirm this suspicion, I was here to end the life of Patrick Bagosora and get revenge for my family and my people. I looked at the pistol I had in my bag. The pistol was registered to me since I was a member of a pistol shooting club, so there was no way for me to claim innocence once I shot Patrick with the pistol.

As I reflected on my plans, I became more and more dissatisfied with them. I couldn't shoot Laurence Juma because of Phillippe's claims. Phillippe was a liar and a con, so I needed to verify Patrick's identity first. After that, I needed to write a manifesto that I could publish. I didn't mind going to jail for murdering Patrick, but it had to serve a purpose. If I could use the trial to bring attention to the plight of my people, I had at least achieved something important.

I entered the office and I spoke to the receptionist. "Hi. I am here to meet with Mr Laurence Juma. He is expecting me."

The receptionist looked at Laurence's diary, shook her head, and replied. "Mr Juma doesn't have any appointments booked at this time. Miss..?"

"Nyamwasa, Samantha Nyamwasa." I replied emotionlessly.

"I am afraid you have to come back another day, Ms Nyamwasa. Laurence is not available." The receptionist replied.

"But I have travelled so far. I must see him today. Can you please make an exception for me?" I pleaded.

The receptionist sighed and replied. "Okay, I'll go speak to him."

The receptionist left, and a short while later, she returned with the irritated Laurence Juma in tow. I looked at the man. He resembled Patrick Bagosora, but I couldn't be sure. I had never spent much time around Patrick, and I had never seen him up close before.

Laurence approached me and grunted: "Miss Nyamwasa. What is so important that you can't book a meeting like everyone else?"

"I am sorry, Mr Juma. My name is Samantha Nyamwasa, and I am working for Tourism Australia. We are looking for a successful African businessman to feature in one of our ad campaigns promoting Australia for wealthy Africans." I replied.

The words that came out of my mouth surprised me. I hadn't planned what to say to Patrick before I had my epiphany in the car, I had only planned to find him and shoot him.

Laurence gave me a curious look and replied, "I see. How come you didn't contact me before coming here? I am sure contacting people in advance is the normal Tourism Australia's procedure."

I decided to reply in Kinyarwanda. Laurence's biography said that he was from Nigeria, so if he understood what I said, that proved my suspicion that he was Patrick. "Nabwirijwe kukubona imbonankubone. Noneho menye ko utunganye kwiyamamaza kwacu kuri Ghan (I had to see you in person. Now I know that you are perfect for our campaign for The Ghan.)" I replied.

Hearing this, Patrick smiled and replied. "I am very flattered by your words, Miss Nyamwasa. Unfortunately, I need to attend a meeting now. Please book a meeting with my secretary, so we can discuss the project further.

"Of course. I am so happy to have you on board with this project." I said and smiled.

Hearing this, Patrick shook my hand and rushed off to his meeting. I smiled as I left the office. I had confirmed that Laurence Juma was a fake identity, and that Patrick Bagosora was alive and well in Adelaide.

Having confirmed Patrick's identity, I went home to plan for his murder. I felt a surge of exhilaration and excitement rushing through me, for the first time in many years. I had loved reading "The Murder on the Orient Express" as a child, and now I could live out the plot of that book while avenging my family and my people.

Chapter 16: Murder on the Ghan; November 2016.

I finished the manifesto where I outlined how Patrick Bagosora had massacred everyone in my Rwandan village. I also provided graphic detail on how he murdered my family. The graphic detail was crucial to get noticed in the 21st-century attention-deficit-world, where mobile devices and social media affected the collective attention span.

I booked the train tickets for The Ghan for myself and Jakob in economy class, and Patrick Bagosora in first class as part of the "Tourism Australia ad campaign" murder plot. It annoyed me that I had to pay for such an expensive ticket for that bastard Patrick Bagosora. However, it was what we had agreed to when I signed him up for the non-existent ad campaign. In the end, it didn't matter. Patrick Bagosora was destined to die on the first day of the trip, so he would have very limited use of his better cabin.

Jakob approached me as I was drinking a glass of red wine, while sitting on the couch in our Adelaide home. Jakob had agreed to come with me as a cameraman, but he didn't know I was going to kill Patrick. I had told Jakob that we would interview Patrick on camera, but that wasn't what I had planned. Instead, I had made an intricate plan where I could commit the murder and be charged with lesser crimes.

Jakob hugged me and spoke, "So, how do you feel about confronting the man who killed your family on camera?"

"I feel a bit tense. I have waited for this moment so long." I replied.

"But what if he doesn't admit to anything, and threatens to sue us for slander? You haven't found any evidence proving that Laurence Juma and Patrick Bagosora is the same person."

"It won't come to that. Trust me, Patrick will swallow the bait." I assured him.

"I wish we could travel without the need for this confrontation," Jakob said.

"Don't worry. We'll enjoy the rest of the trip, after I have confronted Patrick." I lied to him.

Jakob seemed content with my answer. He hugged me tight, and at this moment, I felt closer to him than I had felt for years.

• • • •

WE MET WITH PATRICK Bagosora at the Adelaide train station the following day. Jakob filmed as I interviewed Patrick and made the whole scene to look like a travel promo video. We boarded the train together, and agreed to meet in the restaurant carriage for dinner a few hours later. As I entered my cabin, I started to understand what drove men like Patrick Bagosora. It was an incredible feeling of power to know that I had someone else's life in my hand. I brushed off the thought. I was justified in what I planned to do, because Patrick Bagosora murdered my family and countless of my countrymen. Patrick on the other hand, was a psychopath who killed for the thrill of killing. There was a big difference.

"So, when do you want to do the confrontation scene with Patrick Bagosora?" Jakob asked me as the train started rolling.

"I don't know. I'd rather lead the conversation towards subjects where I would lead him to reveal his true identity. Once we have ascertained our viewers that he is a fraud, we can swing the axe on him." I explained.

"Okay, I hope you know what you are doing." Jakob replied.

I nodded, and a terrible realisation hit me like a tsunami. If I were to kill Patrick on this trip, the police would charge Jakob as an accessory. Why would I risk my poor husband's wellbeing so I could get my revenge? For a moment, I considered scrapping my murderous plan. However, if I did, I would have rewarded my family's murderer with a free weekend of luxury travel. I shook off the idea. I couldn't back down now. I had already backed down from killing Patrick when I decided that I needed to write my manifesto first. My sudden concern for Jakob's well-being was stopping me from doing what I had to do.

I closed my eyes, and I eerily recalled how I suffocated my mother with a pillow to end her suffering. The sadistic monster had left her to slowly bleed to death after raping her with a broken glass bottle, so I had to end her suffering. "Avenge your family, kill Patrick Bagosora." My mother said in my vision.

I knew that my vision was my subconscious talking to me. My mother had never urged me to seek revenge, she had been passing in and out of consciousness and shaking in pain when I found her. Deep inside I knew that my mother, Junema, would never urge me to avenge her death. Junema was a good Christian woman who always spoke about the importance of setting a good example and forgiving one's enemies. Yet I wasn't Junema, and I doubted that God's reason for keeping me alive was to be happy and forgive the past. Too many bad things had happened in my life for that to be achievable.

• • • •

I FELT A SILENT EXHILARATION when I poisoned Patrick Bagosora. As a matter of fact, no-one in the restaurant carriage even knew that it happened. I had stirred down a teaspoon of arsenic in Patrick's Margarita cocktail that he drank while I was interviewing him at the restaurant carriage.

When Jakob went to the bathroom, I leaned in and seduced Patrick. I said, "This has been a very interesting interview, Mr Juma. Would you mind showing me your first-class cabin over another cocktail?" Patrick smiled and replied: "I would love to, Ms Nyamwasa."

As Patrick took my hand and led me to his cabin, I felt a sense of powerful energy. In just a few more minutes, my plan to murder Patrick would begin.

Patrick locked the door behind him as we entered his cabin. He got seated in a luxurious armchair and spoke. "I know who you are, Samantha. I have known since you came by my office."

I tried to sound cool, but I was shaking on the inside as I replied: "Please enlighten me, Patrick."

"Hah! I knew it. You are here because you believe me to be the Rwandan war criminal Patrick Bagosora, who disappeared 22 years ago." Patrick exclaimed.

"Is that so?" I asked.

"Yes. I recognised your Kinyarwanda accent. You are a Tutsi speaker from the Gatsibo region of Rwanda. Your face reminds me of someone, did I meet your mother during the war?" Patrick taunted.

I lost my cool and shouted. "You raped and murdered my mother, along with the rest of my family, you monster!"

"Is that so? Is this silly charade your way of seeking admission of guilt from me? That's never going to happen." Patrick mocked.

"No. I came here to kill you." I replied.

Hearing this, Patrick went into a roaring burst of laughter. Eventually, he spoke: "I am afraid you've trapped yourself, Samantha. I will kill you and leave your body to rot in here. I will get off this train in Alice Springs and fly out of the country. By the time the cleaners find your body as the train reaches Darwin, I will be long gone."

"That's a great plan, but there is a slight problem." I said.

"And what is that?" Patrick mocked.

"I have already chastised you for what you have done to my family and my people. The poison from your cocktail should be in your bloodstream by now." I revealed.

"You're bluffing!" Patrick wheezed in fear.

"Then, try to kill me." I replied.

Patrick tried to get up, but his legs couldn't carry him, and he collapsed to the floor. As he shook in convulsions, I waited for him to suffocate till his last breath, then I put his dead body on the bed and covered his face with the blanket, as if he was merely sleeping. I took his keys, unlocked the door, and left the cabin quietly.

• • • •

THE FOLLOWING DAY, I was drinking cocktails in the restaurant carriage when an alarm went off on my phone. It was time to set the next part of my plan in motion. I excused myself and went to my cabin to fetch my pistol and my phone, so I could livestream Patrick's "murder". I started my phone and I ranted about how Patrick was the incarnation of the devil and how he had murdered my family and my people in the name of satanic powers. I let my pent-up insanity all out. It would help my case later. After ranting for 20 minutes, I walked towards Patrick's cabin. I opened the door, and I filmed myself shooting him with all the bullets in my pistol while he was in his sleep.

Jakob came running towards me and exclaimed: "Samantha, what have you done!?"

"I did it!" I replied coldly.

"You did what?" Jakob exclaimed.

"I killed Patrick Bagosora." I replied.

"But why? Have you lost your mind?" Jakob asked in shock.

"No, he killed my family. I am infertile, and my family ends with me. This is my resolution." I explained.

"So, what are we going to do now?" Jakob asked.

"I will do what Patrick should have done. I will own up to my crimes and accept my punishment." I stated calmly.

I dropped my pistol to the ground, and I sat in silence as I waited for police officers to arrive. I felt at peace as they arrested me and brought me to police custody in Alice Springs. Everything was going according to my plan.

Chapter 17: "The jury finds the defendant to be NOT guilty on the charge of first-degree murder." March 2017.

Thinking back, I don't know what got into me. I was acquitted from murdering Patrick Bagosora, and it is something I have been reflecting on over the years.

A part of me wants to believe it was divine intervention. Jesus had seen how people suffered because of Patrick's action and chose me to be his angel of death. However, for this to be true, Jesus would also have chosen to make me infertile, and stopped me from bringing the Nyamwasa bloodline back. This was what caused me to reach my breaking point. This raised an important question; would the lord of mercy allow a woman to suffer so she could carry out his will as an avenger?

Another theory is that the juries sympathised with my predicament and chose to look the other way. Yes, I had livestreamed my psychotic ramblings when I took a pistol and shot Patrick's already dead body, thus nullifying me from murdering him. However, why didn't they ever conclude that I was the one who poisoned him? There must have been witnesses or security videos that showed how I had drinks with him the day before?

Looking back on the last day of my trial, I remember the relief I felt when the judge read on my final verdict.

It was a steamy autumn day, and the courthouse in Adelaide was full of people. Media from all over the world, particularly from Rwanda, had come to witness the last day of my trial and final statement. My lawyer outlined the crimes that Patrick Bagosora and his uncle Théoneste Bagosora had committed against the Rwandan people. While the United Nations had convicted Théoneste many years earlier, Patrick on the other hand had continued his life of crime, funding terrorism and insurrection by smuggling blood diamonds all over the world. I claimed that I had intended to kill Patrick, but didn't know that he was already dead when I shot him in his sleep.

My speech swayed the juries, and it was a great relief when the chairman of the jury declared that they considered me to be not guilty of Patrick's murder. I did get convicted of a few minor offences, such as a desecrating a dead body and endangering others through firing off a firearm in a confined space. The court sentenced me to two years of imprisonment for my crimes, and of this they deducted the four months which I had been in police custody.

• • • •

I WAS WRITING ON MY autobiography in my cell in Adelaide's Women Prison, when the guard told me I had a visitor. I hoped that it would be Jakob, as we had hardly spoken to each other since the ordeal.

It turned out to be my lawyer and a representative for a publishing house. My lawyer Alice spoke. "Hi Samantha. I was so fascinated by your case, so I ran it by my friend Neil who is running a publishing house."

Neil smiled and spoke, "Hi Samantha. I am Neil Stone from Stone Publishers. I am going to be honest with you Samantha. I haven't read a line of the autobiography you are writing. Yet I know one thing, it will be a bestseller because of all the media attention your case had brought."

I appreciated Neil's honesty. It would have annoyed me if he hid his true intentions for wanting to publish my book. To me, his opinion about my book didn't matter. As long as he published it and the world could read my story, I was happy. I hadn't set out to kill Patrick Bagosora to sell my book, I had done it to avenge my family, my people and to find inner peace. Jesus must have sent this man to help me spread my story, and I would be a fool to reject his help.

I smiled at Neil and spoke: "I would be honoured to work with you and a reputable publisher such as Stone Publishers."

"That's great to hear. I am leaving this contract with you, so you can discuss it with Alice." Neil said and got up.

"Thank you, Neil. I hope to see you soon." I said and smiled. Neil nodded and left the room.

I turned to Alice and spoke, "Thank you, Alice."

Alice smiled and replied. "You're welcome, Samantha. You deserved to catch a break after all the bad things that have happened in your life."

"But you do know that I did kill Patrick?" I asked.

"Of course, I do. I think most people know. But the consensus was to let you off the hook. But never admit in public that you murdered Patrick. That would force the justice system to retake your trial." Alice warned.

"I know. Thank you for looking out for me." I replied.

Alice sat silent for a few seconds. Eventually, she spoke. "I wish you would have come to me earlier. Together we could have convicted Patrick of his crimes and dismantled his diamond smuggling operation. We could have done it the right way."

"I wish that too. Hatred blinded me, and I'll have to live with my actions." I said.

"Well, I guess we are better off looking ahead than dwelling in the past." Alice reflected.

"I agree, my friend," I replied.

We chatted for a while longer. My relationship with Alice had transcended the lawyer-client relationship and I considered her as my friend. I agreed to sign the book deal, and we were excited about the launch that would happen once I left the prison.

I had lied about one thing though. I wasn't regretful that I hadn't contacted Alice before I murdered Patrick. He deserved to die for what he did, and I would have done it all again if I had the chance to change the past.

Chapter 18: A broken trust and an ended marriage; January 2018.

While it should have been a foregone conclusion, I was still sad when Jakob filed for divorce.

It happened near the end of my imprisonment term. I was holding the print copy of my autobiography, and I was looking forward to getting out of prison so I could involve myself in promoting my book. A guard approached me and spoke. "Ms Nyamwasa. Mr Jakob Auma is here to see you."

The guard's words confused me. Why had Jakob introduced himself with his full name instead of telling the guard he was my husband. I grabbed my book and replied to the guard. "Very well. Please lead me to the visitor room so I can speak to my husband.

The guard nodded and he led me to the visitor room. As I entered the visitor room, the guard locked the door behind me, and I faced Jakob, who didn't look happy.

"Hi, Jakob. Is there anything wrong?" I asked.

"I have been thinking about us, and our future?" Jakob mumbled while avoiding my eyes.

"I am listening," I replied.

Jakob sat quietly and I reflected over the future I saw for myself and my husband. Before I murdered Patrick Bagosora, killing my nemesis had consumed my mind. The only future I had foreseen after finding out about my infertility was gloomy and full of death. Now that Patrick was dead, my prospects looked better, yet I hadn't reflected over Jakob's place in my life.

"You broke my trust," Jakob mumbled.

"That's a lie. I have been nothing but faithful to you. I doubt you can say the same." I protested.

My statement silenced Jakob for a while. I knew that he didn't mean sexual fidelity. It had been very easy for me to stay faithful to Jakob as I couldn't have sex without experiencing excruciating pain. It had also been easy for me to look past Jakob's homosexual encounters throughout the years. I couldn't be jealous that he had sex with various men when sex itself was the last thing I wanted.

Jakob spoke again, "I didn't mean that you were cheating on me. I am sorry if my homosexual flings hurt you."

"I wasn't hurt when you slept with others. As a matter of fact, I encouraged it." I replied.

"In any case, this isn't about sex. You broke my trust when you lied and murdered Patrick Bagosora behind my back." Jakob stated.

"I never murdered Patrick, at least not according to the court," I replied in defiance.

"That's because I covered for you. I never told them about how you went with Patrick to his cabin on the day that he was poisoned. That was when you poisoned him, wasn't it?" Jakob speculated.

I shook my head and replied. "No, I spiked the Margarita he drank while we were filming in the restaurant cart. I lured him back to his cabin to avoid having him die in front of everyone."

Hearing this, Jakob slapped me. This shocked me more than any other things in my life. Jakob was weak and effeminate, so I had never anticipated that he would be violent against me.

I thought of punching him, but I refrained from doing so, and instead, I listened to his yappy rant. "You could have told me about your plans. That's how you treat your husband who you have promised to love in thick or thin. Instead, you made me look like an accessory to murder. The cops locked me up for two months. Because of you, I lost my job and our house. I lost everything." Jakob ranted.

I realised that Jakob was correct. I did mistreat him when I obsessed about my single-minded vengeance. For that, I was truly sorry. While I would never apologise for murdering Patrick Bagosora, I should have considered Jakob's well-being when I planned the murder.

"I am sorry, Jakob. I don't know what else to say or do?" I said while crying.

Jakob nodded and handed me some divorce papers. "Please sign this, Samantha. I don't see any future for the two of us."

"Or else what? You fucking coward. You waited for over a year to tell me that it was over between us!" I shouted.

Jakob took a few steps back and he said, "Please don't make this harder than it needs to be, Samantha."

I grabbed the pen, signed the papers, and yelled. "Get the fuck out of here. I don't want to see you ever again."

Without a word, Jakob grabbed the signed document and rushed away.

• • • •

AS MY ANGER SUBSIDED, I felt guilty over how my interaction with Jakob had turned out. He had been loyal to me, and I had repaid his loyalty by harsh words and an angry outburst. I had to come to terms with the fact that I wasn't always the victim in life. I couldn't treat Jakob like that, no matter what Patrick Bagosora, Phillipe, Mbwana Kapombe, and Pesa Nassoro had done to ruin my life. I tried writing a sincere apology letter to Jakob, but I got nowhere. Sorry did indeed seem to be the hardest word to say. At least for me.

I shrugged it off. Although I was a 37-year-old barren divorcee with severe physical and psychological ailments to boot, I still hold on to a slightly better future.

I promised myself that as soon as I had finished my book tour, I would return to Rwanda, buy myself a nice little hut, a little farm and a few live stocks, and live my life as if none of the bad things had ever happened. It was the only way forward. I couldn't change what had happened to me, but I could certainly affect what would happen to me.

"The greatest glory in living lies not in never falling, but in rising every time we fall."

-Nelson Mandela

Chapter 19: Finding peace at last; October 2018.

I was sitting in a beautiful cemetery in the Gatsibo region of Rwanda. I had paid for the remodeling of the graveyard with some of the proceeds from my bestselling autobiography, as my family needed to have a serene resting place. I kneeled next to the family grave and spoke. "I did it, mama. I killed the man who murdered you. I avenged your suffering, and I reminded the world about the plight of our people. I committed the perfect murder. By shooting the dead body of Patrick Bagosora, I convinced the court that I wasn't the one who killed him. In fact, I have murdered him twice. I poisoned him with a lethal drink the day before I shot him, to get away from first-degree murder."

I felt an unexpected breeze coming towards me for a few seconds. It ended as quickly as it appeared. I am certain that my family members' spirits were finally able to go to heaven as I had avenged them. As the wind blew gently, the sun's rays shone through the clouds towards a grave at the end of the graveyard. An adolescent girl was kneeling in front of the grave. I rubbed my eyes in disbelief. The graveyard had been empty when I came in, so where did this girl come from?

I approached the crying girl. She was sobbing in front of a particular grave. I kneeled next to her and spoke gently. "Are you having a tough day?"

The girl looked at me and spoke, "My mother died a few weeks ago. I don't know what to do?"

"What about your father?" I asked.

"He left many years ago. I don't know where he is." The girl sobbed.

"I understand how you feel, my dear. Are you hungry? I can feed and house you while we are looking for your father." I suggested.

"Thank you, Madam. I can't tell you how grateful I am that someone sees me." The girl whispered.

"You'll be safe from now on. I am Samantha." My voice soothed her.

"I am Naomi," Naomi replied softly.

"Nice to meet you, Naomi. We better get you some food." I said, smiled, and took her hand gently.

Naomi smiled and I took her to my place where I prepared a big warm meal and then tapped up a large bath for her.

• • • •

IT IS INTERESTING HOW much one can miss out when one is constantly dwelling in the past. I had walked past Naomi every day for a whole week without noticing her, while my mind was stuck in the past. Once I let go of my dead ancestors, the light shone on Naomi and I noticed her for the first time. I like to believe that Jesus put her on my path, but I am not too sure about it. For that to be true, Jesus would also be the one responsible for Naomi's mother's death, and I rather not host thoughts like that about the Lord of Mercy.

Regardless of why our paths crossed, Naomi turned out to be my second lease on life. Until I met her, I had only lived for myself and avenging for my dead family. Living for the dead is a hollowed existence, and for many years, I was more dead than alive. Once I found Naomi, I got my second lease of life. Together with Naomi, I experienced the happiness that my life entailed before the Rwandan genocide occurred.

At times, I fell back into melancholy. Experiencing happiness and true meaning in life, I bemoaned the many years of sorrow I had wasted. I shook off these feelings as fast as I could. The past was gone, and the future hadn't happened yet, so all that mattered was enjoying the present.

As for Naomi, I found it thought-provoking that she was 12 years old when I found her. This was the same age I had been when the civil war took everything from me. In a sense, I felt like a time-traveller creating a new future for someone walking the same path that I had walked.

I tried to avoid making the mistakes that my adoptive mother in Australia, Lisa Henshaw had made when she raised me. I reminded myself that Naomi was not a replacement for the family I never had. Naomi was a unique gift from God, and the only way I could give her the upbringing I never had, was to treat her as such.

As for Naomi, I am sure that she saw me as a replacement for her dead mother, at least in the beginning. I accepted this for what it was. It had taken me over 20 years to get over my family, and I was selfish if I expected Naomi to change her perspective overnight.

Once Naomi and I had settled in, I focused on my future vision for my village. I prayed to God every night to give me the strength to stay on the path of positivity and love. I had spent too long on my path of vengeance and sorrow, and enough was enough.

Chapter 20: Epilogue; January 2050.

In the grand scheme of things, my death was a happy ending to my last 32 progressive years in Rwanda. Although it felt bittersweet that I never got to watch my great-grandchildren grow up, I guess that is a minor objection, as one can always find a reason to linger a bit longer among the living.

Throughout the years, Naomi and I had been running a charity foundation that was based around looking after orphans and giving Rwandan children a safe upbringing and a good education. It was an issue that Naomi and I were passionate about since we were both orphans ourselves.

Naomi didn't face the same problems I did, and she married a wonderful husband and mothered a few children. I rejoiced at knowing that even though these children didn't bear my bloodline, they still carried on my spirit, and they would bring a brighter future to my country. In the year that I died, one of my grandchildren, Junima, gave birth to a daughter. While I was sad that I wouldn't see this child grow up, it brought me solace knowing that life would go on after my passing.

Although I rejoiced at Naomi's happy family life, it also made me feel bittersweet. I was sad that I couldn't find someone to share my life with, but I had given up on romance after my marriage out of convenience to Jakob failed. Fate had destined me to live alone, and I was better off focusing on how to make the world a better place for those around me, rather than obsessing about my deep loneliness.

The last year of my life, I was getting weary and I had relinquished the control of my foundation to Naomi and her children. I never examined my symptoms, but I believe that I had a rare form of leukemia. I had kept quiet about my condition and I abstained from seeking treatment. There were still lots of young and needy people in Rwanda that needed our help, and I didn't want to bereave them this help so I could live a few years longer.

The day I died, I had been working in my garden, nursing my beautiful plants. My body was weary, but I didn't believe in staying in bed all day. Our bodies were made for movement, so if we bereaved them that movement, we bereaved them the essence of life. Life and living aren't about the number of years, it is about the quality of it. Sacrificing the quality of life to maximise the quantity is a foolish idea based on the unfounded fear of dying.

After a short stint of gardening, I got weary, and I leaned back into a sunchair to enjoy the beauty of my flower arrangements. It saddened me, knowing that I wouldn't be able to see them for much longer, but I longed for coming to the paradise where I would see beautiful flowers yet again and reunite with my first family.

As I watched the sunset behind the vast and majestic African mountains, a bright white light flashed in front of my eyes. Jesus stood in front of me, accompanied by my parents and my brother. I reached for them, they smiled at me, and I became one with the universe.

The End.

Don't miss out!

Visit the website below and you can sign up to receive emails whenever Martin Lundqvist publishes a new book. There's no charge and no obligation.

https://books2read.com/r/B-A-QIOG-IIBMB

BOOKS 2 READ

Connecting independent readers to independent writers.

Also by Martin Lundqvist

Divine Space Gods
Divine Space Gods: Abraham's Follies
Divine Space Gods II: Revolution for Dummies
Divine Space Gods III: Rangda's Shenanigans

La Trilogica Divina Zetan
La Divina Disimulación

Sabina räddar framtiden
Sabinas jakt på den heliga graalen

Sabina Saves the Future
Sabina's Pursuit of The Holy Grail
Sabina's Quest to Open the Portal in the Sun Pyramid
Sabina's Expedition to Stop the Apocalypse

The Banker Trilogy
The Banker and The Dragon
The Banker and the Eagle: The End of Democracy

The Banker and the Empath

The Divine Zetan Trilogy
The Divine Dissimulation
The Divine Sedition
The Divine Finalisation

Standalone
Matt's Amazing Week
James Locker The Duality of Fate
The Portal in the Pyramid
Money Laundering in the Laundromat
Pyramidportalen
Matts Fantastiska Vecka
Divine Space Gods Trilogy
Sabina Saves the Future: Complete Trilogy
Diez Historias Aleatorias y Muy Cortas
Ten Random and Very Short Stories
10 zufällige Kurzgeschichten Volumen 1
Dieci Storie Casuali e Molto Brevi
Dix Histoires Aléatoires et Très Courtes
Cinco Historias Aleatorias y Muy Cortas
Five Random and Very Short Stories
The Fall of Martin Orchard
Masa Depan Putri Sabina
La Caída de Martin Orchard
El Banquero y el Dragón
A Sedição Divina
Dieci storie casuali e molto brevi. Vol 2
Δέκα Τυχαίες και πολύ Σύντομες Ιστορίες Volume 2
The Coldvir-20 Killer
10 zufällige Kurzgeschichten Volumen 2

Förkylningsmördaren
The Banker Trilogy
The Revenge of Blood-Red Rivers
Cha gặp mẹ con như thế nào và suyết chút làm tội phạm giết người

Watch for more at martinlundqvist.com.